The Ghost in the Graveyard

Viola Roberts Cozy Mysteries – Book Nine

Shéa MacLeod

The Ghost in the Graveyard
Viola Roberts Cozy Mysteries – Book Nine
COPYRIGHT © 2020 by Shéa MacLeod
All rights reserved.
Printed in the United States of America.

Cover Art by Mariah Sinclair (mariahsinclair.com)
Editing by Theo Fenraven

Dedication

For everyone who loves Halloween.

We could all use more magic in our lives.

CHAPTER ONE

"Whose idea was this anyway?" I asked, staring into the mirror in horror. A pirate wench with enough exposed cleavage to choke a horse stared back at me. All I needed was an eye patch and a parrot. Maybe a peg leg.

"Bat's. We originally talked about something fancy. Maybe a destination wedding, but neither one of us wanted to wait," my best friend, Cheryl Delaney, said from her nearby perch. The molded plastic chair didn't look comfortable but as usual, she wasn't fazed. "You look super sexy, by the way."

I made a face at my reflection. "I don't think 'super sexy' is the vibe I should be going for at my best friend's nuptials. I'm the maid of honor, not the entertainment."

Cheryl laughed, her dark eyes crinkling at the corners. "Point taken. I should definitely be sexier than you at my wedding. Try the Belle costume. I bet you'll look great."

I returned to the dressing room and slid the curtain shut. "I still can't believe you're having a Halloween wedding. It's not quite how I envisioned your special day."

"Me either," she admitted, "but weddings are ridiculously expensive and stressful, and when Bat brought it up, I thought it would be fun. How can a wedding and Halloween party combo not be a hoot?"

She had me there. I frowned at the wide hoop skirt thing that went with the Belle costume. It was a struggle, but I managed to get it up over my hips.

Cheryl had only been engaged to Detective James "Bat" Battersea for a few months. He'd asked her to marry him during our couples' trip to Oregon wine country. I thought we'd have more time to plan, but Bat had vacation time he needed to use, they'd gotten a steal on a package to Greece for their honeymoon, and they'd both been in complete agreement that there was no point diddly-farting around—Bat's words, not mine.

"Have you decided on your costume?" I asked.

"I'm the bride," she said as if that explained everything.

"Sure," I agreed, voice muffled as I dragged a bright yellow dress over my head. "But this is a Halloween party. For all I know, you're coming as Morticia Adams."

"Hardly. I'm wearing a bridal gown, which we need to shop for, by the way."

I repressed a groan. "Do you have any idea how long it takes to get a wedding dress ordered?"

"Not a used one. We can visit some consignment shops and see what they have. My mom can tweak it."

Cheryl's mom, Charline, was a whizz with a sewing machine. She could make or fix just about anything with a swatch of fabric and a bit of thread. I had no doubt she could redo whatever we bought into something gorgeous, even if it was a 1980s prom reject.

"What about Bat?" I asked.

"He says it's a surprise, which has me worried, but he looks good in anything, drat the man."

"That's trued." I turned to look in the mirror. Oh dear. Talk about prom rejects. "I— Oh. This is not— Oh no. Cheryl, I can't wear this. Not to your wedding. Not anywhere."

"Let me see."

I stared at my reflection. "I don't want to come out."

"Viola Roberts, come out this minute, or I'm coming in to get you."

I sighed heavily. "Fine."

Shoving the curtain aside, I stepped out and braced myself. She burst into peals of laughter. Tears ran down her face, and she had to cross her legs.

"Just for that, I'm wearing this to your wedding," I threatened.

"That is the worst thing I've ever seen," she finally sputtered.

She wasn't wrong. The dress was made of cheap satin fabric that was incredibly shiny. The bright yellow made my pale skin with its pink undertone look sallow and sickly. It stretched tightly over my boobs, straining so the fabric pulled awkwardly. The princess waistline showed off the fact that I enjoyed donuts a little more than I probably should, and the hoopskirt made me look about a hundred pounds heavier than I actually was. If that wasn't bad enough, whoever had designed the thing thought putting mutton sleeves on it was a grand idea. They puffed up and out, making me look like my head had been swallowed by a beehive. It was... terrible.

"The pirate outfit was better than this hot mess," I grumbled. "I'm going as Gandalf. I can throw on a robe and be done with it."

Cheryl was still laughing, her brown skin flushed with humor. "There's got to be something better than that. I have an idea! Instead of some crazy costume, why not wear something retro. Like from the '50s or something. You'd look great in a fit-and-flare dress. Then you can add vintage pieces, like a handbag and shoes. You could be Donna Reed or Della Street."

I perked up at that. "I could totally be Della Street. I loved her in *Perry Mason*." Growing up, I'd watched all the black and white reruns on TV. It had been one of my favorite shows. I'd always loved mysteries, especially when the bad guy always got caught. It was a surprise to everyone when I decided to write historical romances instead of murder mysteries.

"Well, get out of that hideous thing and let's go check the charity shops for wedding dresses and vintage looks," Cheryl ordered.

"Yes, ma'am."

It was a struggle, but I managed to worm out of the Belle dress and back into my usual jeans and sweater. My stomach rumbled, letting me know I hadn't had anything to eat since a bowl of cereal that morning, and it was now nearly two.

"Let's get some food," I suggested as I exited the dressing room. "I could use a break and some sustenance."

"Me, too," Cheryl said. "We'll grab a bite at Blue Delicious, and after we finish shopping, we'll treat ourselves to wine at Sip."

"This is why we're best friends," I said, linking my arm with hers.

Blue Delicious was located a few blocks up from Main Street, where I'd been trying on costumes.

It was located in an older brick building that was painted blue. Swirling letters spelled out the shop name across a large plate glass window that gave a good view of the Columbia River below.

The minute I opened the door, the yeasty scent of fresh-baked bread wafted out, and my stomach growled again. I inhaled deeply. It reminded me of when I was a kid and Mom dropped me off at Grandma's for the day. Grandma always had something in the oven: bread, biscuits, cookies—you name it. My love affair with carbs started early.

The girl behind the counter probably wasn't even eighteen yet. She wore a pair of jean overalls, and her black hair was done in pigtails that made her look twelve. There was a silver hoop in her right nostril, thick black gauges in each ear, and a colorful sleeve of astrological tattoos on her left arm. Pretty typical of most coffee shop and bakery workers in the area. I didn't recognize her, so she must be new.

"Welcome to Blue Delicious. What can I get you?" the young woman asked perkily.

Cheryl grinned. "Hi, Stella. How about a bowl of tomato soup and a grilled cheese sandwich?"

Figured Cheryl would know her. She knew everyone in town. She'd grown up in Astoria while I had moved here only a few years ago.

"Sure thing, Ms. Delaney." Stella rang up Cheryl's order and turned to me, eyebrow lifted. There was a silver barbell through the eyebrow.

"I'll have a turkey, brie, and chutney on whole wheat," I said, eyeing the pastry case. "And a lemon tart."

"Speaking of tarts," said a woman behind me. "If it isn't Cherry Delaney."

Cheryl spun around, scowling. "It's Cheryl, Tiffany. As you well know."

After paying Stella and putting my tip in the jar, I turned to get a look at Tiffany. She was pretty much what I expected: tall, thin, bleached blonde. She'd probably been a cheerleader in high school. All the Tiffanies I'd gone to school with had been. and by all, I meant three. Yes, there were three girls named Tiffany in my graduating class. Meanwhile, I'd gotten stuck with a name like Viola. Terribly old fashioned back then, but I liked it now. It suited me.

This particular Tiffany had definitely seen better days. There were those tiny vertical lines around her mouth that betrayed her early smoking days, though she didn't smell like smoke now. The crow's feet and forehead creases were surprisingly deep for a woman in her mid-forties. The color of her hair, which probably hadn't changed since 1992, didn't help. It left her features looking harsh and ragged, as did the thick, black eyeliner and frosted pink lip gloss. I wasn't sure if she was one of those women that still used the same makeup she'd used in her heyday or if she had simply embraced the resurgence of the '80s look that had become all the rage.

Makeup and hair aside, Tiffany did not look happy. It looked like life had kicked her in the teeth more than once, and it had turned her hard and bitter. I felt sorry for her until she opened her mouth.

"Still slutting around with Bat?" Tiffany sneered.

"We don't slut shame in this town." I swear I channeled my inner sheriff. There was a reason I wrote historical romances.

Tiffany turned a gimlet eye on me. "Who asked you, fatso?"

Once upon a time, that rather pathetic comeback would have hurt, but I was older and wiser. Well, at least older. I'd learned to embrace who I was, including my not-insubstantial curves. I was no longer the awkward girl I'd once been. My self-confidence had been hard won, and I wasn't about to let this mean woman put a chink in it. I didn't know what her problem was, but I wasn't going to let her get to me or hurt my best friend.

I gave Tiffany a long, blank stare and then I turned away as if she meant less than zero. "Hey, Cheryl, let's sit by the window. We'll get a nice view of the river."

Stella, who'd been staring open-mouthed through the exchange, cleared her throat. "I'll bring over your food when it's ready."

"Thank you, Stella," Cheryl said.

"Yes, thank you." I stuffed an extra five-dollar bill into the tip jar. Stella deserved it.

Tiffany snarled something nasty under her breath, but Cheryl and I ignored her as we crossed to a rustic wood table next to the window. After hanging our coats on the backs of the chairs, we sat but didn't relax until Tiffany had gotten a loaf of breath and stormed out, the door banging shut behind her. She stomped past the window, middle finger raised. We ignored her.

After she vanished around the corner, we both nearly wilted with relief.

"I could sure use that herbal tea," Cheryl muttered.

"I could use something stronger than tea," I said. "What was that all about?"

"She and Bat dated in high school. He was on the baseball team, and she was a cheerleader."

No shocker there. It was pretty much what I'd expected.

"Bat was super popular in high school. Not like me. I preferred theater and yearbook. Stuff like that."

"High school was decades ago. Surely she's not that pathetic."

"Sadly, she is. After high school they went their separate ways. He attended the university, got his bachelor's degree, then went on to the police academy. She married the former captain of the football team, who lost his scholarship after blowing out his knee and became the high school football coach."

And town drunk. I remembered. "He died the year I moved to Astoria, didn't he?"

She nodded. "Drunk driving. Wrapped himself around a tree. He wasn't dead a month before she was throwing herself at Bat. He wasn't interested."

More than likely because he'd had a crush on Cheryl even then, and who could blame him? "Still, her reaction was over the top. She's taking this mean girl thing too far."

Cheryl shrugged. Stella approached our table with a tray filled with goodies. She set it down, gave us a wan smile, and returned to her spot behind the register.

"Poor kid. No doubt she puts up with crap like that all the time." I plucked my sandwich off the tray and took a bite. It was delicious, the chutney adding a nice tang. I'd discovered chutney while visiting England with my boyfriend, Lucas Salvatore, and had been a fan ever since. I was glad to see it was making its way to this side of the Pond.

"It is kind of crazy," Cheryl admitted. "I've never done anything to her. We weren't friends or even enemies. She totally ignored me in high school and that was, well, a lot of years ago. I don't get it."

"Maybe she's a little... you know." I waffled my hand back and forth.

"Unbalanced?"

"Maybe she's not taking her meds or something. It happens. Or maybe she's not drinking enough water."

"You think she's mean because she's dehydrated?" Cheryl took a bite of her sandwich.

"Remember when your mom's neighbor went nuts and streaked through the neighborhood in her birthday suit? They said it was dehydration."

"Mrs. Sweeny is eighty-five years old. Lack of water doesn't effect a forty-something the same way."

"Still, could cause an electrolyte imbalance or something. Or maybe she's just mean as a snake."

"I'm going with the latter," Cheryl said. "I've known Tiffany a long time, and she's never been nice to anybody except Bat. Every time she's around him, she simpers like a 1950s starlet."

"Are you going to tell him?"

"What, about Tiffany being a jerk? What's the point? It'll just piss him off, and there's nothing he can do about it. She didn't break the law."

"Well, she was a big meanie."

She giggled. "What are you, five?"

I grinned. "Subject change. Have you decided where to get the cake?"

"We were thinking Bakeology. Sandy does such a great job decorating, and her cakes are so moist and yummy. We're thinking chocolate cake with dark chocolate frosting draped in spider webs."

Ew. I was not a fan of spiders, even in frosting. "You're really going all out with this Halloween theme thing, aren't you?"

"Why not? In for a penny, in for a pound. Sandy can make one tier cake and then a bunch of cupcakes and cookies. That way there's a variety of flavors for everyone: lemon, vanilla, pumpkin."

"Sounds delish. I'll have one of each."

"I'm stumped on the flowers, though."

"Decorations or bouquet?"

"Decorations for the tables."

"Easy. Just get those cute teensy pumpkins everybody uses these days and turn them into centerpieces with whatever flowers and greens are available. Autumn leaves. That kind of thing."

"Perfect!"

We chatted through lunch about wedding plans, but I couldn't get the confrontation with Tiffany out of my mind. It had felt like more than just a mean girl attitude. It had been personal, and I couldn't help the worry that niggled away at me the rest of the day.

CHAPTER
TWO

"That woman!" Bat exploded. "Someone ought to do something about her."

It was later that evening, and Cheryl and I had joined Bat and Lucas on an exploratory mission. We had an appointment to see a lovely bed and breakfast that Cheryl found online. It promised to be the perfect venue for the Halloween wedding. We'd barely settled in the car when Bat started ranting.

"I take it you mean Tiffany Carlson," Cheryl said. "How'd you find out about that?" She slid a look at me.

I shook my head. I hadn't told him. I hadn't even had a chance to tell Lucas.

"Stella told me when I went in to grab a late lunch at the bakery," he said.

Well, that explained it.

"What's going on?" asked Lucas, who'd missed the excitement.

I gave him a quick rundown on what had happened at Blue Delicious. "It was weird how rude she was to Cheryl. It was an unusual amount of hostility for someone you've barely seen since high school and over what? The fact she dated Bat for five minutes? Really, Bat, I thought you had better taste."

Cheryl stifled a giggle.

Bat gritted his teeth. "As you well know, Viola, I do have better taste. People do stupid things in high school." It was clear he thought dating Tiffany had been a stupid thing, and I couldn't agree more.

"Let's put it out of our minds," Cheryl said. "She's not important. She can say whatever dumb thing she wants about me. We know the truth."

"Yes, we do," I agreed. "You're awesome, fantastic, smart, successful, and beautiful."

"Aw, you're making me blush."

"Is that it?" Lucas asked, peering through the windshield.

"Yes! Isn't it amazing!" Cheryl gushed.

Amazing was certainly a word for it. The elegant Queen Anne, situated on top of a hill with a good view of the Columbia River, had been painted in various shades of black and gray, from pale silver to deep charcoal. The only hint of color was the front door, which was blood red.

"It certainly fits the theme," Lucas said as we all clambered out of the car. "It's the kind of house where bodies are buried in the cellar."

"I like it," Bat said, and that was the end of it.

Until I saw what was beside the property. "Is that a graveyard?"

"Cemetery," Cheryl said. "One of the oldest in the state. I think it gives the place atmosphere."

"You're getting married, Cheryl. Not, uh, the other thing."

"Buried?" She rolled her eyes. "Of course not, but it's *Halloween*. It should be fun."

"Sure, okay. You're the boss."

The woman who opened the door was nothing like what I expected. I was thinking a Lily Munster type. You know, all goth, all the time. But she was a short, round, grandmotherly type with tightly permed gray hair, Mrs. Brady glasses, and a frilly mint-green apron over a pink track suit. Her house slippers were hot pink and sequined. She had to be in her eighties.

"Hello! Welcome!" she shouted. "I'm Mrs. Ermengaard, but you can call me Bev. Welcome to Raven House. Come on in!"

The entry hall was snug, not really big enough for all of us to cram into at once, and decorated in red flocked floral print wallpaper. A small black crystal chandelier hung in the center. The floor was black and gray checked. It also smelled like fresh-baked chocolate chip cookies.

"I've got cookies in the oven," Bev said as if reading my mind. "But let me show you around first." She led us through a formal dining room, also done in shades of black and gray, to a surprisingly cheerful white and red breakfast room. "I was thinking this would be a perfect space for the ceremony. I know it's small, but we can open up the dividing doors and put additional chairs in the dining room."

"It's perfect," Cheryl gushed.

"Nice view of the cemetery, too." Bev pointed. Outside the window several grave markers leaned haphazardly alongside a low, wrought iron fence. "We can put hurricane lanterns with tea lights near some of the stones. Make it nice and spooky. Come this way, and I'll show you where we'll hold the party."

The "party room" was actually a cavernous formal living room. It was red and black, like just about everything else, right down to the crimson velvet sofa and the dark gray gargoyle perched on the black marble mantel.

"You've got an interesting color scheme going," I said.

Bev chuckled. "Not my taste really, but you gotta cater to your audience."

"Is your bed and breakfast popular with the goth crowd?" Lucas asked.

Or vampires?

"Yes, but not so much for the decor. The place is haunted."

Cheryl let out an excited squeal. "There's a real ghost?"

I was about to tell her ghosts weren't real when Bat spoke up. "Several. I read about it online. One is supposed to be the original owner, I believe."

"Yes." Bev beamed at him. "James Johnson. He built the place in 1886 and lived here with his wife, Maude. James liked to dip his quill in the company ink, if you get my meaning, so Maude whacked him over the head with a rolling pin. Lights out!" She was awfully cheerful about it. "They say Maude is here, too, still chasing him with that rolling pin."

"There's another ghost, too," Maude said. "While this house was being built, one of the workers fell off a ladder and died. Very tragic. His wife, in her grief, jumped off the roof to be with him."

"Well, that's a bit much," I muttered.

Bev ignored me. "It's said she haunts the cemetery next door, searching for her lost love. So romantic."

Not how I would have put it, but nobody asked me.

Raven House didn't seem like a great place to start married life, what with all the dead couples, but what did I know? Plenty of people got married in churches and divorced a year later, so I supposed where you tied the knot probably didn't matter nearly as much as who you married. I glanced at Lucas. That was definitely something I should keep in mind.

The day of the wedding was, as is typical of Oregon, overcast and drizzly, but the meteorologist promised it would clear up in time for trick-or-treating. I reminded myself to leave a bowl of candy on the porch since I wouldn't be there to hand it out. That was too bad. I loved seeing the neighborhood kids in their costumes.

I met Cheryl and her mom, Charline, at Raven House. The front porch was decorated with an animatronic witch who cackled and stirred her cauldron when someone walked by.

Bev had set aside the honeymoon suite so we could get ready, and she had fresh baked snickerdoodles and mugs of steaming Thundermuck! coffee. The snickerdoodles were even better than the chocolate chip cookies from our first visit.

We were joined by the ladies of our bunco group. Bunco was a fun dice game and several of us got together each month to play. Over the years we'd all become friends. We spent the day draping the house with fake cobwebs and setting carved pumpkins across the porch. .

"This is the most ridiculous thing I've ever heard of," Agatha, one of the bunco ladies, said to me as we decorated a black Christmas tree with purple bat-shaped twinkle lights.

"You don't like the idea of a wedding on Halloween?" I asked.

"It's not the date that's the problem," she said. "It's the theme. Please don't tell me she's wearing a black dress."

"She's not." I didn't tell her Cheryl's white dress was identical to the one worn by Princess Leia during the awards ceremony at the end of *Star Wars: A New Hope.* She would probably assume, since it was white, it was a regular old wedding dress.

By the time we finished decorating the house and getting ourselves ready, it was twilight and we still hadn't put out the lanterns. I was surprised the groundskeeper was allowing it, but Bev assured me he'd given the okay as long as we collected them afterward. "Don't worry," I assured Cheryl, "The sun's still up. Agatha will help me light them, and I'll put them in the cemetery."

"Good," Agatha said, "because I'm not walking around a graveyard after dark."

Once the tea lights were lit, I carried the lanterns through the open gate and set them around the stones nearest the house. The idea was to give them spooky up light. Since the stones were the real deal, Cheryl thought it was better than buying cheap foam ones from the craft store.

I'd just placed the last one when I caught something from the corner of my eye, like a swirl of white disappearing from view. I turned my head, but whatever it was had gone. If it had ever been real in the first place. Maybe the Raven House ghosts had followed me.

I told myself not to be an idiot. I was letting my imagination run away with me.

I started back to the house but found myself looking over my shoulder. "Ghosts aren't real," I muttered out loud.

I could have sworn I heard someone laughing.

CHAPTER
THREE

The wedding was surprisingly magical. There was no other word for it. A local Wiccan practitioner performed the ceremony was dressed as a fairy, complete with wings and a crown of fresh flowers. She even added neat little touches like a handfasting, complete with ribbon, to symbolize their commitment.

Bat's parents were there and really got into the spirit of things, with Mr. Battersea dressed as Spock's dad, Sarek, and Mrs. Battersea as Spock's mom, the human Amanda Grayson. They wore full Vulcan finery and looked splendid. Charline was glorious in a gorgeous, flowing Greek goddess outfit complete with gold sandals and laurel crown. She was the perfect Hecate. The bunco ladies and Bat's friends from the police department mostly wore classic witch, superhero, or animal costumes they'd picked up from the Halloween shop.

I was decked out in a 1950s evening gown I'd found online and had rush delivered. It had a snug bodice and an even snugger skirt, as I'd gone for a wiggle-type dress rather than a fit and flare. Lucas wore a dark suit of the same vintage, which basically made him look like a darker, sexier James Bond.

After the vows were exchanged, the pronouncements made, and the kiss sealed the deal, everyone went to the party room, where the cake had been set up, along with the cupcakes and cookies. The cake was exactly as Cheryl had described it, with dark chocolate frosting and white spider webs draped over it. Sandy hadn't added spiders, but the cake topper looked like boy and girl mummies kissing.

I couldn't believe my best friend was married, and to a hunky police detective to boot. It was surreal.

Everyone gathered around the main table, where Bat and Cheryl prepared to cut the cake. Charline was snapping away with her cellphone while Bat's dad pulled out an honest-to-god video camera. What was this, the nineties?

Lucas tapped a butter knife on the side of his champagne flute and got everyone's attention. "Friends and relations, welcome! On behalf of Bat and

Cheryl, I want to welcome you and thank you for coming. And now, what we're all really here for!"

There were scattered giggles. All eyes swung toward newly married couple, glasses and cellphones ready.

"Okay, you crazy kids, cut that cake!" Lucas ordered.

Flashes strobed as Bat and Cheryl took hold of the knife and pressed it through the bottom layer of cake. Everyone cheered as they removed a thick slice of dark chocolate cake and fed each other a bite before drinking from each other's glasses. Naturally the champaign flutes were black with little rings of orange crystal beads around the stems.

Bat lifted his glass. "Thank you for coming. Cheryl and I—"

He was interrupted by a blood-curdling scream from the kitchen. Everyone froze.

I slammed my glass on a nearby table and charged to the kitchen. Well, it was more a shimmy than a charge. My skirt was ridiculously tight.

Bev was standing at the sink, staring out the window, face ashen. A broken plate lay on the floor, and she was shaking so bad, I thought she might keel over any minute.

"Bev, what's wrong?"

She pointed. "Th-there's a body out there."

"Don't you mean a ghost?" I said sarcastically, stepping around the broken china to join her.

"I-I don't think that's a ghost."

The window gave me a good view of the cemetery. The hurricane lanterns lit the gravestones with flickering, eerie light. I expected to see someone flitting around in a bed sheet. Instead there was a form slumped on the ground halfway between the gate and the nearest stone marker.

"Is that—?"

"A body," Bev whispered. "It wasn't there a minute ago. I went to get more plates from the pantry, and when I came back—" She gestured helplessly.

I snorted. "Probably somebody got into the champagne early. I'll go check on them."

I opened the back door and went carefully down the wooden steps, then picked my way across the lawn on tiptoe so my heels wouldn't sink into the soft earth. The gate stood open—I hadn't bothered closing it after placing the lanterns as I'd just have to come out and collect them again—and I stepped through and knelt next to the figure. Though her back was to me, it was clear from her hair and figure it was a woman. She wore what looked like a wedding dress, complete with veil and tiara. How bizarre. Halloween costume maybe? Although it was inappropriate to dress as a bride for a wedding when you weren't one.

I shook her shoulder gently. She reeked of booze. "It's time to wake up now. Party's not over yet."

She didn't move. In fact, she was so unnaturally still, it gave me the heebie-jeebies. I swallowed hard, suddenly not wanting to know if she was drunk or dead. Couldn't someone else check on her? Where was everyone?

Something white flitted in my peripheral vision, and I jerked my head up. Whatever it was, it was gone. I shook my head and turned back to the matter at hand.

"Miss? Ma'am?" I touched her hand. It was cold and clammy, and I felt for a pulse in her neck. Nothing.

Dread pooled thick and ugly in my stomach, and I suddenly felt ill. I took a deep, steadying breath and glanced back at the house. The yard was still empty. Everyone else had heard the scream. Why was I alone out here?

I turned back to the woman. "Please don't be dead."

I grabbed her shoulder and turned her onto her back. Her hair streamed out on the grass, and her hand flopped to her side. Open eyes stared blankly at the sky.

It was Tiffany Carlson, and she was definitely dead.

Turned out the reason no one had come to my rescue was that Bev fainted and everyone had freaked out. It had taken some time to realize that not only was I missing, but the the back door was wide open. Only then did Cheryl poke her head out and see me hunkered over someone in the cemetery. She immediately sent Bat.

I sat on the bottom step of the back porch with an afghan around my shoulders while Bat directed the crime scene people. I'd made a mess of it, of course, but in my defense, I'd thought she was alive. Dead drunk, maybe, but not actually dead.

"How are you feeling?" Lucas asked, sitting next to me and handing me a mug of steaming hot coffee.

I took a sip and realized it was spiked with whiskey. No doubt for shock, except I was pretty sure I wasn't in shock. A shiver passed through me. Okay, maybe I was.

"I can't believe this happened on Cheryl's wedding day," I murmured. "During Cheryl's wedding."

"You didn't answer the question."

"I'm fine. I think. Ask me again tomorrow."

He wrapped an arm around me and tugged me close. "Will do. What happened?"

"No idea. When I heard Bev scream, I ran to her, and she was staring out the window like she'd seen a ghost. That's when I saw Tiffany, only I didn't know it was her yet."

"Who?"

"Tiffany Carlson, the woman we ran into at the bakery, remember? The one who dated Bat a million years ago. She was mean and nasty, but she didn't deserve to die. Do we know yet how that happened?"

"Looks like a blow to the back of the head," Bat said as he approached the house.

Maybe I really was in shock. I hadn't even noticed him coming. "I didn't see an injury. There wasn't any blood."

"It was under the wig."

"She was wearing a wig? I hadn't realized," I said with a frown. Granted it was dark, and both her hair and wig were blonde, but it seemed like that was a thing that would have stood out. Then again... shock. "Are you investigating?"

Bat shook his head. "Since it happened more or less at my wedding, it'll get turned over to Baker." He beckoned to a woman who stood nearby. "She'll have questions for you. I'm going to go check on Cheryl."

As he left, Detective Baker walked over. She was in her late forties or early fifties. Her dark hair was cut into a neat bob that accentuated her high cheekbones and wideset, angular eyes.

"Detective Ruth Baker," she said, stepping forward and shaking first my hand, then Lucas's. "Just joined the force. Moved here from Salem."

"Welcome to Astoria," I said.

"Thank you. You're the one who found the body." It wasn't a question.

"Yes." I told her what I'd told Lucas about finding Tiffany.

"Did you see anyone else? Hear anything?" Detective Baker asked. She was no-nonsense and to the point. I liked her.

"Well, sort of."

She perked up. "Explain."

"Um, well, I caught something out of the corner of my eye. Movement. A flash of white. But when I looked up, whoever or whatever it was, was gone."

Her eyes narrowed. "Whatever?"

I cleared my throat. "They say the place is haunted. Ghosts running amok."

She snorted. "Surely you don't believe that."

"I don't, but other people do, and it *is* Halloween."

She snorted. "Ghosts don't kill people."

"Never said they did, but I'm betting whoever dressed up as a ghost was either involved or saw something. Why else would they run away?" I pointed out.

"Don't you worry. I'll have my people comb the cemetery."

"Good. You might find some clues."

She rolled her eyes. Actually, she was too professional, but I could tell she wanted to. "The victim. I understand you knew her?"

"I wouldn't say I knew her. More like I had a run-in with her."

Baker's eyes narrowed. "Tell me about it."

I realized how I'd made it sound, but there was nothing I could do about that but tell the truth. "Like I said, I didn't really know her. I was at Blue Delicious with a friend a couple of weeks ago, and she came in after us. She was pretty nasty."

"Nasty how?"

Reluctantly, I told Baker what Tiffany had said to Cheryl, followed by what Cheryl had told me. I didn't like the speculative gleam in Baker's eyes.

"Your friend went to school with the victim?"

"Yeah, like half the rest of the town, including Bat, and I think she was mean to most of them. In fact, Bat dated her at one point." I threw Bat under the bus without a thought. If someone was going to prison for this, it wasn't going to be my best friend. Not that I wanted it to be Bat, but he was a cop. He could handle himself with Baker.

"Bat?" Baker asked.

"Detective Battersea," I clarified.

"Right." She tapped on her phone screen, taking notes. "But the victim didn't attack Detective Battersea. She attacked your friend."

"And Bat's wife," I pointed out.

She gave me a thin smile. "Of course. Where can I find Mrs. Battersea?"

I almost snorted. Cheryl as Mrs. Battersea? That was hilarious. "Ms. Delaney is inside. She's the one sort of dressed like a bride."

Baker's eyebrow went up. "Sort of?"

"You'll see."

CHAPTER FOUR

I followed Baker inside, but when I would have joined her in the front room with Cheryl, she firmly shut the door in my face. Rude, but not surprising. Police were usually funny about letting civilians in on their interrogations.

Cheryl had a pretty solid alibi, as did Bat and everyone else at the wedding, what with being in a room together. Photographs and videos would show that no one had left the room once the cake cutting started. Baker would soon find herself looking elsewhere. I might as well make myself useful and search for clues to point her in the right direction. But first I needed to change. My dress was too snug for traipsing around a graveyard, searching for a supposed ghost.

I'd changed with Cheryl in the honeymoon suite on the second floor but then moved my things to one of the smaller bedrooms on the third floor, since Bat and Cheryl would be making use of the suite after the ceremony. Bev had assured me the third floor was practically empty at the moment, leaving me free to pick whatever room I liked. I'd gone with the black and purple vampire-themed room.

At the top of the third-floor stairs beneath a window that looked out over the cemetery was an old steamer trunk painted black and topped with a skull resting on a doily. Because why not? Only something was weird, and it took me a moment to realize what was off.

When I'd come up earlier, the trunk had been latched and the skull and doily perfectly centered. Now the latch was loose, the trunk lid slightly wonky, and the doily and skull were off-kilter.

I studied it closely, trying to figure out what the problem was. I realized that the edge of a bit of white fabric was just visible between the seam created by trunk and lid, as if someone had quickly stuffed something into the chest without making sure the lid could close all the way.

I've never considered myself nosy, but curiosity overwhelmed me. I set the skull and doily on the windowsill and lifted the chest lid. I don't know what I'd expected to find inside—a skeleton maybe—but it was full of musty old copies of *National Geographic*. Most of them looked to be from the '70s. Wadded up on top was what looked like a white sheet.

I pulled it out and held it up. Someone had cut two eyeholes in it, like something straight out of *Peanuts* or *Scooby Doo*. Could this have been worn by whoever had been running around the cemetery?

I inspected the sheet carefully. Sure enough, there were green grass stains along one side, as if whoever wore it had sat on the grass. Waiting for someone? Or spying? My guess was that this was from whoever I'd seen out in the cemetery. But there wasn't a speck of blood, so perhaps they were not the killer. But they'd hid their costume in the chest, which indicated they probably thought they'd be blamed for the murder.

That brought me to another thought. As Bev had told me, the third floor was pretty much empty.

No guests outside the wedding party. The ghost couldn't be just anyone, given the chest was on the third floor and out of sight from the rest of the house. It had to be someone who not only had access to the house, but who would have gone to the third floor to hide their disguise. I guessed it was someone familiar with the house, which pointed to Bev.

But it was Bev's scream that alerted us to the murder. How could Bev have been in two places at once?

She couldn't be, of course. Which begged the question: Was there someone else involved in whatever this was?

Shaking my head, I wadded up the sheet and took it downstairs with me. I probably shouldn't have touched it. I should alert Baker so she could have the techs look for DNA or whatever, but I didn't want an innocent person getting blamed. Plus, I was the only one who'd seen the alleged ghost, I couldn't be sure this belonged to that person.

Bat and Lucas were in the kitchen, drinking coffee and munching on pumpkin-shaped sugar cookies. Bev was nowhere to be seen. Bat looked grim and Lucas worried.

"Cheryl still with Baker?" I asked.

Bat nodded. "She'll be fine. Baker's a good detective, and Cheryl has an alibi."

I showed them what I'd found. "I think it belongs to whoever I saw in the cemetery."

"You think this is the 'ghost' everyone's talking about?" Lucas asked.

"I think it was tonight," I said.

"You should give that to Baker," Bat said. "You're messing with evidence."

"Am I?" I asked lightly. "I'm not even certain of what I saw. For all I know, this has been in that chest for ages."

Lucas snorted, blue eyes dancing with laughter. "I believe you."

I grinned. "I think it's Bev, but I don't know how or why."

"Bev was here," Bat pointed out. "She's the one who alerted us."

"But she could have followed me outside. Played ghost."

Bat shook his head. "She fainted, remember? Lucas and I had to move her because she fell in front of the door. That's why it took us a while to get to you."

"Oh. Right. Good point." Who else could it have been? I held up the sheet, suddenly realizing something. "There's no mud."

"What?" Lucas asked.

"On the hem of the sheet. No mud." I showed them. "This sheet is big enough that if Bev had worn it, it would have dragged along the ground. The cemetery is soggy. There would have been mud."

"We already established it couldn't have been Bev," Bat said.

"But here's the thing, it's too long for me, too." I showed them. Sure enough, when I draped the sheet over my head, it dragged on the floor. I removed it. "In order to avoid getting mud on the sheet, the wearer would have had to be significantly taller than me. By several inches at least."

Bat took the sheet from me. "By six inches or more."

"Right, so five eleven. Which means it was either a very tall woman—"

"Or a man," Lucas said.

I nodded. "The sheet is too big for Bev, but what do you want to bet she knows something?"

"Or someone," Lucas mused.

Bat's expression turned grim. "I think we should find out."

Bev was in her office next to the stairs doing paperwork. She had apparently recovered from the shock of seeing someone lying on the ground in the cemetery. Maybe I was being unkind, but why would she scream just seeing a woman lying on the grass? I could understand her screaming over a dead body— that was a shocker—but how could she have known Tiffany was dead? I hadn't known until I took her pulse, and I'd been standing over her.

Unless Bev had seen something, like the ghost. Even more likely, she could have planned the whole thing with the ghost.

I tossed the sheet on the desk. "Hey, Bev, look what I found."

She stared at the sheet, her face nearly was white as it was. She gave a nervous laugh and slid her pen behind one ear. "It's a bed and breakfast. There are a lot of those around. A whole closet, in fact."

"Not like this. This one has holes in it." I held it up so she could see.

She cleared her throat and glanced at Bat. "I'm afraid that'll come out of your deposit."

Bat snorted. "I wouldn't try it. None of us cut holes in that sheet."

"I'm betting it was Bev who cut the holes," I said. "Or whoever she's in cahoots with."

"I-I don't know what you mean."

"Don't you?" Lucas said.

"Of course she does," I said. "She had to have. I found this particular sheet shoved in a chest on the third floor. Since the rest of the guests are either staying at their own homes or on the second floor, none of them would even know about the chest on the third floor."

"They could have gone poking around and found it," Bev pointed out a little shakily.

"That's true," Lucas agreed. "Except all of us have an alibi."

Bat nodded. "That's right. Every single person at the wedding was in the living room for the cake cutting when the murder took place. We have pictures and videos to prove it."

"Every one of us," I reiterated, "except for you, Bev." Granted, I hadn't seen the pictures, but she didn't know that.

"I was in the kitchen, as you well know." She set her jaw.

"Sure," Lucas agreed. "We know you were, but your partner wasn't."

She crossed her arms. "My husband has been dead for twelve years, and there is no one else."

"You sure about that?" Bat asked. "I think I should speak to Detective Baker. Let her know what's going on."

"No! Don't do that. Please," Bev begged. "He didn't do it. I'm sure of it."

"Who didn't do it?" I asked, leaning a hip against the edge of the desk. "Who wore this sheet and why?"

She seemed to almost sink in on herself. "My nephew, Garrett. He's a good boy, though. A kind boy. He didn't kill anyone. I'm sure of it."

"Then why was he running around a graveyard dressed like a ghost?" I asked.

She put her head in her hands a moment, then straightened, shoulders back, resolved. "When my husband passed, all I had left was this big old house, so I turned it into a bed and breakfast. It was something I'd always dreamed of, and I really enjoyed it. At first I did really well. Every weekend was booked solid through the summer. Even in the off-season, I was busy. But the last few years... well, things changed. It was getting harder and harder to get people in. The bills were piling up. The place needed repairs. I was getting desperate."

"And then?" I prodded.

"Then my nephew Garrett came to visit. Technically he's my great-nephew. He had the idea about the ghosts. He saw it on some television show."

"I think you'd better clarify that," Bat said.

She twisted her hands together. "He said we needed a UPS."

I blinked. "Do you mean a USP? A Unique Selling Point?"

"Oh yes, I think that's it. He said just being a nice place to stay wasn't enough, and every Victorian bed and breakfast from here to Maine was all about gingham and romance."

I wasn't sure that was true, but I kept that to myself. "Go on."

"He thought the place had the right atmosphere to be haunted. It's not, of course. Ghosts aren't real, but people like to think they are, I guess."

"What about that stuff about the original builder dying here and haunting the place?" I asked. "Even Bat knew about that one."

"Only because I read it on her website," he admitted.

Bev shrugged. "The house is old. I'm sure lots of people have died here, but nobody's stuck around that I can tell. Makes for some good stories, though."

"Is Garrett responsible for the, ah, decor?" Lucas asked.

She nodded. "He thought it would appeal to the sort of people we were trying to attract. He even came up with the ghost stories."

"Did it work?" I asked.

"At first. We were busy. People came from all over to stay at the haunted bed and breakfast with their gizmos and psychic powers and whatnot. They'd hold seances in the dining room and set up cameras in the basement." Her shoulders sagged. "But when nothing exciting happened, they left and didn't come back, and told their friends the place wasn't haunted."

Which meant she had a kitschy house on her hands where no one wanted to stay. "Is that when

Garrett decided to play ghost and make something happen?"

"Yes," she admitted. "At first it was only here in the house. Mostly things like knocking on walls, items moving, doors suddenly opening and closing."

"All easy things to rig," Bat mused. "A bit of fishing line, a recording. Easy."

"Which is what some of the guests claimed. They weren't terribly impressed." Bev sighed. "Garrett said we needed to up our game. That's when he came up with the idea for the ghost in the graveyard."

"Catchy," Bat said dryly.

"He invented a story, and I was supposed to tell the guests. One night during their stay, I'd get them into a location where they could see the cemetery. He'd put on the sheet, get some dry ice going, and walk through the grave markers. We even practiced and got it to the point where it was really convincing."

"And you decided to pull your prank at our wedding?" Bat demanded, brows lowering.

"It seemed like a good idea at the time. Lots of guests meant plentiful word of mouth. I desperately need the money more guests would bring." She gave him a pleading look, which he ignored.

"Where is this nephew of yours?" he demanded.

"I don't know!"

"Did you see what happened?" I asked. "With Tiffany, I mean."

She shook her head. "I looked up and saw him running across the cemetery toward the bushes at the back, and that woman was just lying there. I didn't know what to do, so I screamed."

Seemed like a weird reaction to me, but it's hard to say how people will react in a stressful situation. I once caught a fit of the giggles while I was on jury duty. "Garrett must have come back to the house, since his costume is here."

"He could have come in through the side door, I suppose. That's the door that leads to my apartment. There's access from there into the main part of the house, but I haven't seen him. I swear."

"We'd better tell Baker," Bat said. "We're going to need to find him."

"He didn't kill that woman," Bev insisted. "He would never harm a fly. He was only trying to help me."

"And yet a woman is dead," Bat said grimly. "Your nephew has a lot to answer for."

I nodded. "Guess we're going ghost hunting."

CHAPTER
FIVE

Detective Baker wasn't thrilled about the wedding guests participating in the "ghost hunt," but she didn't have much choice. There weren't enough police to handle the search, and time was of the essence. Not to mention, half of them were already roaming around the house and yard, searching for clues.

"Besides," I pointed out, "he's probably not dangerous."

Her brow arched. "Not dangerous? He might have killed a woman."

"I said 'probably.'"

"Oh, no, he would never have done that," Bev insisted. "He's a very sweet boy. He wouldn't harm anyone. He doesn't even like killing spiders."

"I'm in," Agatha said. She was wearing a Wonder Woman costume, complete with tiara. "And I'm armed." She held up her handbag, also Wonder Woman themed. Knowing her, it probably weighed twenty pounds. She carried an entire pharmacy in there. Everyone in Astoria knew if they needed anything, from an antacid to a hairpin, Agatha had it somewhere in the depths of her purse.

"I think we should go in pairs," I suggested. "For safety's sake."

"Good idea," Bat agreed.

I was stunned he was going along with this. Usually he tried to stop me from investigating things. Marriage already agreed with him.

"I'm with Viola," Cheryl said. She was still wearing her Princess Leia gown.

If Bat was disappointed she wanted to go with me instead of him, he didn't show it. He gave her a quick kiss, then he and Lucas climbed the stairs to the attic. Agatha and Charline went to poke around the detached garage. Baker and her officers took the rest of the house and grounds, including the basement.

"Where should we search?" Cheryl asked.

"The cemetery. That was the last place I saw him. He might still be there."

"Except he came back long enough to hide the sheet," she pointed out. "Do you really think he would have risked sneaking past the police to return to the scene of the crime?"

"Why not? It's probably the last place they'd look for him."

"What do you mean?" she asked as we picked our way across the squishy lawn.

"The police searched the cemetery right after they saw the body. Why would they bother doing it again?"

"So you think after he hid the sheet in the house, he waited, then when the police finished searching the cemetery, he went back and hid?"

"Makes sense to me. There's a good view of the cemetery from the third-floor landing window. It's unlikely anyone would have noticed him watching, and with everything so chaotic, he could easily have slipped back out and hidden again right under our noses."

We passed through the still open gate. Crime scene tape fluttered in the breeze, but it appeared the techs had finished gathering evidence. Since Baker hadn't posted a guard, she must have felt it was pretty safe.

At the back of the cemetery was a lopsided shed that had seen better days. I figured it was where they kept the lawnmower and other gardening tools. It was the perfect hiding place, since Baker had already searched it. Garrett could wait there until everyone left, then sneak back to the house.

"Get your flashlight ready," I whispered to Cheryl.

She pulled up the app on her phone. Finger hovering over the button, she gave me a nod.

The door was unlocked, and I flung it open. "Aha!"

Cheryl pressed the button on the app and shone her light around. Only there was no sign of Garret. The place smelled of must and gasoline. Dust and cobwebs were thick in the corners, a pair of shears hung from a hook on the wall, shelves were lined with bottles and boxes of bug spray and plant food, and a cheap lawnmower was in the middle of the concrete floor. Off in one corner was a stack of old twelve-gallon paint buckets. Otherwise the place was empty.

"Got any more bright ideas?" Cheryl asked sarcastically.

I backed out and shut the door. "What's that?" I pointed at a chain-link fence blocking off a corner of the cemetery which looked older than the rest and was partially overgrown.

Cheryl squinted. "No idea. Looks like they're refurbishing some of the grounds."

"Let's check it out."

Easier said than done. There was a double gate, clearly meant to admit a vehicle, which was chained and padlocked. I didn't see any other way in.

"Guess we've got to climb the fence," I said.

"Are you nuts?" Cheryl hissed. "This is private property. You can't go climbing fences willy-nilly. Besides, you'll break your neck."

"No I won't. I'm a champion climber."

She snorted. "Climbing stairs doesn't count."

"Don't be ridiculous. I'm talking trees."

"When you were, what, ten? You're forty—"

"I may be forty something," I cut her off, "but I haven't forgotten how to climb a tree. It's like riding a bike."

"I don't think that's true."

"Besides, a chain-link fence is a lot easier." I rammed the toe of my shoe into one of the wire openings, grabbed onto the fence and hauled myself up. "See? Easy peasy."

"This is nuts. There is no way Garrett climbed this fence without anyone seeing him."

I kept climbing. It was only once when I reached the top that I realized the fence was awfully high, and I wasn't entirely sure how to get down the other side. It was too far to drop, so there was nothing for it but to get down the same way I'd gotten up, which meant somehow swinging around, straddling the top bar—without gouging myself in the hooha— and situating myself for the climb down.

"Easy peasy," I muttered through clenched teeth. Cheryl was right. I was too old for this nonsense, but there was no way I was admitting that now.

I managed to swing my right leg over the top rail and hover there long enough to find a toehold.

Now for the left. I started out fine, but then my jeans pocket snagged on the mesh, and I was stuck. No matter how I pulled or pushed, I couldn't get loose.

"Cheryl, a little help here."

"You look ridiculous."

Her voice came from below, but not from outside the fence. I looked around to find her staring up at me from inside it like I was a moron.

"How'd you get in there?"

"I walked through the gate." She pointed.

I craned my neck. Sure enough, on the section of fence that ran parallel to the vehicle gate was a people-sized gate, and it was wide open. "Oh bother."

She smothered a giggle. "I think you might have to take off your pants."

"I am not taking my pants off!"

"Why not? No one is looking. Once they're off you can get them loose."

That was how I ended up standing in the middle of a cemetery in my knickers. I glared at Cheryl, who was laughing so hard, I was afraid she might split a seam. "You said I could get them loose when I was out of them, but that is not the case." I jabbed a finger at where my jeans dangled from the mesh.

"I guess you snagged them harder than I thought," she said between gales of laughter.

"I cannot hunt for ghosts in my skivvies," I complained. "I will freeze my tookus off." And probably get arrested for indecent exposure or something.

"Then go up and get them."

"I already scraped the bejeesus out of my butt cheek," I said, showing her where the mesh had scraped a welt along my left cheek and upper leg. It hurt like the dickens, and it was going to be hard to explain to Lucas.

"Fine, I'll go." She was up like a cat, snatched my jeans free, and was back down before you could say, "Bob's your uncle." And she'd done it in a Princess Leia gown. Maybe she was channeling Carrie Fisher's pluck.

After I put my jeans back on—and Cheryl had stopped laughing—we prowled the fenced off area until we came to a pile of dirt next to a backhoe. Next to the pile of dirt was a long trench.

"Help?" someone said.

We peered over the edge. The trench was about six feet deep. A pale face under a shock of red hair gazed back at us. He looked about eighteen but was probably in his mid-twenties.

"Let me guess," I said. "You're Garrett, Bev's nephew."

"Our ghost," Cheryl supplied.

He had the grace to look shamefaced. "Yeah. Can you help me out?"

"I'll grab one of the buckets from the shed." Cheryl dashed off. She returned shortly and tossed the bucket in the hole. Garrett was able to use it like a stepstool, and between the three of us, we managed to heave him out of the hole.

"Are you going to turn me in?" he asked when we'd gotten our breath back.

"I don't want to," I said, "but you sort of killed a lady."

"Hardly a lady," Cheryl muttered.

"I didn't mean to," Garrett said.

That caught me by surprise. "You really killed her?"

"It was an accident," he insisted. "I was doing my thing—"

"Playing ghost," I pointed.

"Yeah, but that was only to help Aunt Bev. It was the only thing I could think of to save her place, and it was working."

"There you were, in the cemetery, playing ghost, and then what?" I prodded.

"I stumbled on that blonde lady. She was drunk and talking about burning Aunt Bev's house down—"

"She was going to burn down the house?" I asked. "Why?"

He shrugged. "I'm not sure. She kept ranting about teaching people a lesson not to ignore her."

Cheryl and I exchanged glances. Whoops. I was the one who'd ignored her. If that had made her mad enough to burn down a stranger's house because we were in it, she'd needed help, and that made the whole thing sad, actually.

"What happened next?" Cheryl asked.

"I thought I'd better call the cops, but she grabbed me and started screaming about me disrespecting her and weird stuff like that. I was so freaked out, I pushed her away and ran. I guess she fell and hit her head on one of the stone markers, but I didn't realize it until it was too late. I didn't mean to hurt her, I swear."

"Then why did you hide when the police came?" Cheryl asked.

"I was scared," he said. "I don't want to go to jail."

Cheryl and I exchanged looks. I felt bad for the kid. Tiffany had been a terrible person, but she hadn't deserved to die, even if she had been planning to burn down Raven House. Garrett seemed like a nice kid, and he didn't deserve to go to prison. What a mess.

I sent Lucas a text to let him know we'd found the "ghost" and to tell Baker. I got a text back immediately, saying she was on the way.

"I'll talk to Bat," Cheryl told Garrett. "He's a detective. Maybe there's something we can do."

"That's awfully nice of you," Garrett said. "I'm real sorry."

"Next time maybe don't play ghost," she suggested.

"Hopefully there won't be a next time," I said. "I'll talk to your aunt. I bet we can come up with a way to help her."

He brightened. "Would you really?"

"Sure."

Baker was charging across the cemetery toward us. Poor kid was about to have a rough time of it. Helping his aunt was the least I could do.

"Don't worry, the kid will be all right," Bat assured me.

It was the next morning, and Bat, Lucas, and I were waiting for Cheryl by the front door of Raven House. It had been late by the time Baker let us go. Too late for them to leave on their honeymoon, though Baker had given the go ahead, so we were doing the whole bouquet toss/birdseed throw thing this morning.

"How can you be sure?" I asked. "They arrested him for killing someone."

"It was an accident. I'm sure forensic evidence will bear that out. He'll have to pay for what he did, but the fact it wasn't done on purpose will be taken into account, as will Tiffany trying to burn the house down."

While Tiffany's blood alcohol level had been sky high, part of the boozy smell on the body had been from a broken Molotov cocktail, which supported Garrett's claim Tiffany had been hell-bent on causing problems.

"Seems like an overreaction from an old girlfriend," I pointed out.

"I called around," Bat said. "She'd been dating Vic Hargrave. He went to school with us. Anyway, turns out he wanted to break up, but she wasn't getting the hint. In order to get rid of her, he claimed he had a new girlfriend and led her to think it was Cheryl. He didn't realize Cheryl and I were together. He was just trying to get Tiffany to move on."

"And she thought Cheryl had stolen two men from her," I mused. "She probably thought everyone was against her. I almost feel bad for her."

Lucas snorted. "Almost? She was going to burn down Bev's B&B. Bev never did anything to her. She was just mad she wasn't getting her own way."

"She clearly had problems," I said, "but she didn't deserve death, nor does Garrett deserve to go to prison for an accident."

"He won't," Bat assured me. "My guess is it'll be ruled self-defense. For one thing, Tiffany Carlson attacked him. For another, he's got a clean record and a good defense attorney, thanks to you. He'll be fine."

That was a relief.

Bev bustled out from the kitchen with a stack of plastic storage containers. She thrust them at us. "My little way of saying thank you. I can never repay you for what you've done for me and my nephew, but I thought chocolate chip cookies might be a start."

"They're more than enough in my book," I said. "What will you do now? Will you keep running the B&B?"

"I'm getting too old for this stuff. I think I'll retire. Move closer to the family. Monday I'm going to ring the real estate office and put this place on the market."

Cheryl came down the stairs, a big smile on her face and a bouquet in her hands. "Ready?"

The guys backed up, and Bev waved goodbye and returned to the kitchen. Cheryl turned her back and threw the bouquet. Naturally it landed squarely in my arms, which wasn't difficult as I was the only person standing there.

When she reached the ground floor, Bat took her hand and Lucas opened the door for them. I instantly recognized the car parked at the curb, and it wasn't Bat's.

"Is that the Batmobile?" I asked, laughing at Bat's grimace. I often teased him by calling him Batman. He hated it.

Lucas grinned. "Yep. The one from the TV show. I rented it for the day. Thought it would make a fun wedding present."

"I approve," I said.

"Thought you might."

They got in, and the car roared down the street and turned the corner. Lucas and I stood on the porch, arm in arm, enjoying the view of the river below, and the town that stretched down the hill toward it.

In that moment, I realized I enjoyed being with him more than anyone else. Maybe even more than Cheryl. While I wasn't ready to get married yet, I thought it was time we took our relationship to the next level.

"We should move in together."

He turned to look at me. "Are you serious?"

"Yes. What do you think?"

He grinned. "I think it's a great idea, except I'm not sure either one of us has room for the other."

That was true. My Victorian cottage was small, as was his condo by the river. We needed a lot more space if we were going to make this relationship work.

"We'll sell our places and buy something together." I glanced at the blood red door. "I heard this place is for sale."

He laughed. "Only you would want to live in a haunted house."

"I ain't afraid of no ghosts."

 THE END.

Did you enjoy Viola's latest adventure? Then you might enjoy my other cozy mystery series: *Lady Rample Mysteries* (set in 1930s London), *Sugar Martin Vintage Mysteries* (set in post WW2 era England), and *Deepwood Witches Mysteries* (modern day paranormal cozies with witches and magic).

A Note from Shéa MacLeod

95

Thank you for reading. If you enjoyed this book, I'd appreciate it if you'd help others find it so they can enjoy it too.

Please return to the site where you purchased this book and leave a review to let other potential readers know what you liked or didn't like about the story.

Book updates can be found at www.sheamacleod.com

Be sure to sign up for my mailing list so you don't miss out!
https://www.subscribepage.com/cozymystery

You can follow me on Facebook https://www.facebook.com/sheamacleodcozymysteries/ or on Instagram under @SheaMacLeod_Author.

About Shéa MacLeod

97

Shéa MacLeod is the author of the *Lady Rample Mysteries*, the popular historical cozy mystery series set in 1930s London. She's also written paranormal romance, paranormal mysteries, urban fantasy, and contemporary romances with a splash of humor. She resides in the leafy green hills outside Portland, Oregon, where she indulges her fondness for strong coffee, *Ancient Aliens* reruns, lemon curd, and dragons.

Because everything's better with dragons.

<u>**Other Cozy Mysteries by Shéa MacLeod**</u>

Lady Rample Mysteries
Lady Rample Steps Out
Lady Rample Spies a Clue
Lady Rample and the Silver Screen
Lady Rample Sits In
Lady Rample and the Ghost of Christmas Past
Lady Rample and Cupid's Kiss
Lady Rample and the Mysterious Mr. Singh
Lady Rample and the Haunted Manor
Lady Rample and the Parisian Affair
Lady Rample and the Yuletide Caper (Coming December 2020)

Sugar Martin Vintage Cozy Mysteries
A Death in Devon
A Grave Gala
A Christmas Caper

Deepwood Witches Mysteries
Potions, Poisons, and Peril
Wisteria, Witchery, and Woe
Moonlight, Magic, and Murder
Dreams, Divination, and Danger

Viola Roberts Cozy Mysteries
The Corpse in the Cabana
The Stiff in the Study
The Poison in the Pudding
The Body in the Bathtub
The Venom in the Valentine
The Remains in the Rectory

The Death in the Drink
The Victim in the Vineyard
The Ghost in the Graveyard

<u>Non-Cozy Mysteries by Shéa MacLeod</u>

Intergalactic Investigations (SciFi Mysteries)
Infinite Justice
A Rage of Angels

Other Books by Shéa MacLeod

Notting Hill Diaries
To Kiss a Prince
The Art of Kissing Frogs
Kiss Me, Chloe
Kiss Me, Stupid
Kissing Mr. Darcy

Cupcake Goddess Novelettes
Be Careful What You Wish For
Nothing Tastes As Good
Soulfully Sweet
A Stich in Time

Sunwalker Saga
Kissed by Blood
Kissed by Darkness
Kissed by Fire
Kissed by Smoke
Kissed by Moonlight

Kissed by Ice
Kissed by Eternity
Kissed by Destiny

Sunwalker Saga: Soulshifter Trilogy
Fearless
Haunted
Soulshifter

Dragon Wars
Dragon Warrior
Dragon Lord
Dragon Goddess
Green Witch
Dragon Corps
Dragon's Angel
Dragon Mage

www.ingramcontent.com/pod-product-compliance
Lightning Source LLC
Chambersburg PA
CBHW021021160726
47994CB00006B/2609